I Wonder Who Hung the Moon in the Sky

yeah!

Mona Gansberg Hodgson
Illustrated by Chris Sharp

CPH
SAINT LOUIS

Written for my friend Jerri Ann Knister. I remember the first time I heard Jerri clap for God. It was during a sunset displayed on the red rocks of Sedona, Arizona.

I Wonder Series

I Wonder Who Hung the Moon in the Sky

I Wonder Who Stretched the Giraffe's Neck

I Wonder How Fish Sleep

Text copyright © 1999 Mona Gansberg Hodgson
Art copyright © 1999 Concordia Publishing House
Published by Concordia Publishing House
3558 S. Jefferson Avenue, St. Louis, MO 63118-3968
Manufactured in the United States of America

1   2   3   4   5   6   7   8   9   10   08   07   06   05   04   03   02   01   00   99

A Note to Parents and Teachers

The *I Wonder Series* will delight children while helping them grow in their understanding and appreciation of God. Readers will discover biblical truths through the experiences and whimsy of 7-year-old Jared.

This book, *I Wonder Who Hung the Moon in the Sky*, provides a playful exploration of our world and God's character while centering on scriptural truth. The activities on pages 30–32 will help children apply and practice the truths revealed in Jared's imaginative investigation of creation.

As you read this book together, share these Bible words with your child:

In the beginning God created the heavens and the earth. *Genesis 1:1*

Enjoy!

Mona Gansberg Hodgson

Hi! My name is Jared. I live in Arizona.

Do you ever wonder about things? I do.

I wonder when I hear the wind whistle. I wonder when I see a shooting star fall through the night sky. Everything makes me wonder.

Last week my grandpa came to live with us. I call him Papa Ray.

On Saturday morning, I helped Papa Ray mix pan- cake batter for  breakfast. That's when I asked him where things come from.

After we ate I asked, "Did the world come out of a box just like pancakes?"

Papa Ray showed me what the Bible says. It says God created the sky and every- thing in it. The Bible also says God created the earth and everything in it.

Then, the Bible says, God created people to help Him take care of His wonderful world.

That's a lot to make! How did He do it? I wonder.

I saw a huge crane move
a box to the top of a building.
Do you think God used a

really big crane to hang the
moon in the sky? I wonder.

My dad said, "God would
not need a crane. God can
just speak and things move
into place."

God is amazing!

11

Papa Ray wears red suspenders to help him hold up his pants. Do you think God uses suspenders to hold the planets up in the sky? I wonder.

My mom said the planets stay where God wants them to because He is the one who created them. I think she's right.

At night, when my mom and I lie on our backs in the grass, we see at least a gazillion stars twinkling. Do you think they're winking at God? I wonder.

Maybe the stars wink because they're glad God made them. I'm glad God made me. I wink at God too.

14

When I play outside, dirt creeps under my fingernails. At a picnic, dirt flies onto my peanut butter sandwich. Do you know why God made dirt? I wonder.

My dad says flowers and trees grow in dirt. I like flowers and trees.

I'm glad God made dirt. Aren't you?

The wind blows the leaves into the air. When I feel the wind blow, I know that God is all around me. How do you think God made the wind? I wonder.

Papa Ray told me God has  always been here, even before the world. He said God will always be with us, even until forever. I wonder if God has a birthday party every year. That would be a lot of birthdays!

Maybe God makes the wind by blowing out His birthday candles. What do you think?

It started raining during our family picnic. Why does it rain? I wonder.

Clouds don't stub their toes. Clouds don't laugh at jokes. Why do you think clouds shed tears?

I think God created clouds so they would send down rain to water His plants. What do you think?

Have you ever seen a rainbow? How does God put so many colors in a rainbow? I wonder.

My mom gave me some colored chalk so I can draw pictures on the driveway.

Does God use colored chalk to create rainbows? What do you think?

23

The saguaro is a kind of cactus that grows near my house. Saguaro cactus have branches that look like arms. Why did God put arms on the saguaro cactus? I wonder.

My dad says some birds build their nests in the saguaro's arms. It's amazing how God takes care of all of us! Don't you think God is amazing?

25

Where I live there are lots of mountains made of rock. Have you ever touched a rock? Why are rocks so hard? I wonder.

I think maybe God made rocks hard so He could use them as building blocks for mountains. What do you think?

27

I like to wonder, don't you? When I wonder, I think about God. I like to think about God. I like to thank God for all the great things He made.

In the beginning God created the heavens and the earth. *Genesis 1:1*

Thank You, God, for making the whole, wide, wonderful world.

Thank You, God, for being my Creator and Savior.

Thank You for being my amazing God! In Jesus' name. Amen.

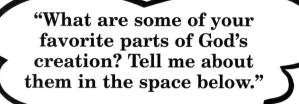

"What are some of your favorite parts of God's creation? Tell me about them in the space below."